# COME RAW

Lars Rasmussen

SERVING HOUSE BOOKS

Come Raw



Serving House Books logo by Barry Lereng Wilmont

ISBN: 978-0-9825462-2-2

Published by Serving House Books

www.servinghousebooks.com

First Edition 2009

# Foreword

Lars Rasmussen is a man of many parts: He has owned and managed an antiquarian bookshop in the center of Copenhagen, The Booktrader, for over twenty years now. As a publisher, he has issued excellent and rare works on South African jazz, golf and other topics as well as a CD recording series which includes both jazz and many of the greatest living poets in Denmark. And he has published many books of his own stories, not to mention his annual Christmas journal containing fiction, poems, essays, and art by many of his customers — and he does have some impressive customers who include writers, musicians, artists, singers, actors, journalists, professors, and most of all, readers.

The Booktrader is a very special place, a unique place, where you will meet a book dealer who knows his stock, and the shop on any given day is a nest of fascinating conversations between Lars and his customers, many of whom are themselves fascinating people. Lars himself has been interviewed and written about in many venues.

What a pleasure for Serving House Books to be the first American publisher to make available a collection of Rasmussen's writing - which, as readers will see, defies genre classification. His influences? A bit of Hans Christian Andersen, a touch of Rimbaud and Verlaine and Baudelaire and Poe and others more contemporary as well as a great deal of Lars Rasmussen who is always, first and foremost, uniquely himself.

Welcome to his world of strange, haunting tales, sometimes lyrical, sometimes dark as deep Danish winter night, and sometimes both, and sometimes all of these things. There is even a story here written in Latin! Although it is followed immediately by the English version. Whether brief as a flaming match or burning more slowly, like a taper in the dark, these tales have a tendency to brand themselves into the reader's mind.

Turn the page and step into an imagination very much its own.

—*Thomas E. Kennedy,* for Serving House Books

Lars Rasmussen

photo by Birte Gerner Larsson

Lars Rasmussen's other titles in English
*A Ghost of 9/11*
*If God Could Speak*
*Confessions of a Fox-Buddha*
*The Sublunary World*
can be purchased from www.booktrader.dk.

# CONTENTS

# HANS HANSSEN, SAILOR

Hans Hanssen is my name. I am a sailor, born 1842, in the southern part of Jutland, the peninsula that rises from the northern coast of Germany like a slightly curved, warty index finger, and makes up almost half of the kingdom of Denmark. I come from a family of seafarers. Many of my ancestors were whalers and, as a child, I was never in doubt that I was to be a sailor. I dreamed of being a captain, the master of my own ship, though I never managed to get so far. But even as a simple sailor, occasionally a ship's cook, I can't complain about my life. I have traveled all over the world and experienced everything a sailor in the age of the tall ships could ask for. I have seen distant and exotic countries, and I can tell about typhoons, shipwrecks, and strandings; about pirates, smugglers and cannibals and, indeed, I often do so, to anyone who is ready to listen. And if no one else cares to lend an ear to these stories, at least my grandchildren always will.

But there is one story I have never told anyone, for the simple reason that it lacks the outer drama that my listeners expect from a good story, and it lacks a proper ending. It will, as it seems, always remain an unsolved riddle. Now that I have the chance to put my thoughts on paper, I want to tell that story, of my meetings with a most unusual and enigmatic person, whose true identity I have never been able to establish. Allow me to start somewhere in the middle, with the third of our four meetings, since that was the only occasion on which I got the chance to actually talk to him.

In August 1876, when I had been stranded in the Javanese city of Samarang for a couple of weeks, I was lucky to ship out as cook on a small Scottish vessel, *The Wandering Chief*, bound for Europe with a cargo of sugar. The Captain was Scottish, Brown was his name, and we were a crew of nine men, all Europeans, for the most part from the British Islands.

It was a jolly company; I was soon nicknamed 'the wandering chef,' and everybody onboard got on well with each other. It was the most pleasant trip right up until we reached the Cape of Good Hope, where we encountered a terrible storm. The ship nearly capsized and we had to cut away three masts to right her, and part of the cargo was washed away. After two terrible days and nights, when we all feared for our lives, we were able to sail peacefully on to Europe.

There was one person onboard who especially attracted my attention. His name was Edwin Holmes, and he claimed to be one of the few survivors from a vessel named *The Oseco,* which had been abandoned in the Indian Ocean a month before our departure. There had been a lot of talk in Samarang about the rescue of *The Oseco's* crew, and Holmes, who was a true story-teller, gave a dramatic account of the events. He was a tall and strong man, deeply browned by the sun, but even though he could swear, work hard, and get dirty from work like all the other sailors, he sometimes revealed a double nature, as if in fact he was a gentleman, traveling incognito. There were several things to support this suspicion.

Now, I am by no means an expert in the English language, but I had at that time sailed between Esbjerg and Newcastle for nearly ten years, and, consequently, met a lot of Englishmen, of all social classes, and I was quite certain that this man spoke excellent English, but with an accent which could only be that of a Frenchman. When I heard him pronounce my name, there was little doubt left.

It was, of course, none of my concern that this person, the company of whom I had come to appreciate very much, had reasons to pretend he was someone else, and I had absolutely no interest in finding out what those reasons might be. What I had in mind was to find out whether he was identical with a Frenchman I, by fate's strange intervention, had happened to see twice before in my life.

One morning, as we were both standing on the deck watching the seabirds, I dared approach him about the matter.

*Vous êtes français, n'est-ce pas, monsieur?*

I'm sorry, but I prefer to speak English!

I know, but you *are* French, aren't you?

Don't you find my English satisfactory? He looked scornfully at me.

Of course I do. It is much better than mine, I know that all too well. It is the way you pronounce my name that gives you away. And there is one thing more: I believe I've seen you before. Twice, in fact. A year ago, there was a French circus, *Cirque Loisset,* in Copenhagen. It gave a number of performances, and I went twice to see it, once with my family, and once with some friends. It was a very good circus, there were some very funny clowns, and they had the most fierce wild animals in cages, but I was especially impressed by the remarkable *sprechstallmeister* who spoke six or seven languages fluently. Even with your sunburn and different haircut, I would certainly say the man looked exactly like you.

He didn't answer. I continued:

But when I saw that *sprechstallmeister,* or ring master, as I believe the English say, I was certain that I had seen him before. I came to Paris in 1871, as a young sailor on leave, and I got very much attracted to the night life. I used to frequent a certain Bohemian hang-out on Place Pigalle, called *Le Rat Mort*, an all-night café which attracted many poets and painters. Everybody seemed to smoke hashish, and here I first tasted absinthe. My French at that time was terrible, but I understood it better than I spoke it. A certain evening I remember this so vividly a young, gangling poet, whom I had noticed a couple of times before, walked in. He was, as it always seemed to be the case, accompanied by an older man, and they immediately became the center of everybody's attention.

After a few drinks, the young man stood up and read aloud, from a much worn manuscript which he pulled out of his pocket, a long poem. I no longer remember any of the words, but it made a deep impression on me. It was about a drunken boat. *Le Rat Mort* was usually a very noisy place, but it was all quiet while the young man was reading, and I remember his very distinctive voice. He may have had a bit of a country dialect; that I can't tell for sure, with my limited knowledge of the French language, but he definitely spoke in a way like no one else. Then, when he had finished reading, there was enormous applause, followed by animated drinking and discussion. I noticed that the other poets, even those much older than he, and more famous, never seemed to be jealous of him. That poet was definitely identical with the ring master I saw four years later in the circus, and I would be very much surprised if you will now deny that you are that very same man!

I am sorry, but I am a sailor, not a poet, he answered. And I have never traveled with a circus. It is quite an exotic story you are telling me, and I would certainly love to be able to speak seven languages fluently, but I am afraid I only master my own language, which is English. And if I fail to pronounce your name properly, I must ask you kindly to forgive me, but it is not a familiar name, not even to an Englishman.

With these words he excused himself and retired to his berth. I was left alone on the deck.

From that day he kept a certain distance to me, and I regretted I had disturbed him. He had been better company than the other crew members.

Years passed, but I never forgot that elusive person whose path through life had kept crossing mine so mysteriously.

In May 1891 I happened to find myself in the harbor of Marseilles, having a few days off while my ship was waiting for its cargo to arrive. One day I noticed some crew members on a ship which had arrived that same morning from Aden, carry a sick man ashore, while others were watching. He was lying completely flat on a stretcher, looking up in the air, and he didn't notice me. I don't think he was able to notice anything other than his pain, which was obviously great. He was in fever, mumbling in French. Only a few words were recognizable: 'tusks ... muskets ...' The man was incredibly sunburnt, and very enervated. I did, however, immediately recognize him as my strange acquaintance from *The Wandering Chief.*

As I stood next to the ship and watched the man being carried into an ambulance, one of the crew members approached me.

That man has come here to die, he said in French. It's a matter of days. We brought him here from Aden, and we were afraid he wouldn't make it to his native country. *Cancer,* he added, and gave me a meaningful look.

I can see he is in bad shape, I replied. It may sound strange, but would you happen to know if this man is a poet?

*Un poète? Non, monsieur, au contraire,* he was a tradesman. A great one. Ivory and weapons, some even say slaves. He is only 36. A pity that he must die so young!

A great pity indeed.

I spent the rest of the day, and much of the evening, walking up and down the streets of Marseilles, musing over this man who seemed to have lived at least four completely different lives within one short lifespan, seemingly always denying his previous incarnations. I wished he hadn't been so afraid that I wanted to pry into his life. All I really wanted was once again to hear that poem, which had impressed me so much that night in Paris, the poem about the drunken boat.

I desperately kept trying to remember just a few lines, but to no avail.

## BONSAI

It is a warm late summer's day in the Meiji Old Peoples' Home in Tokyo's northern outskirts. In the lounge facing the gardens sit three wizened figures, each in his own wheelchair; everything about them is distorted; their legs, faces, arms, hands, backs. One of them has had both legs amputated. Every now and then the staff appears to rearrange their pillows or serve them green tea in porcelain bowls.

On tables around them stand the most beautiful bonsai trees.

I do not understand it, says one of them with a bitter grimace. I have not harmed a living soul in my life. Why should I end up like this? Sometimes it occurs to me to curse Buddha and to wish him and his teachings to hell. What sort of karma is this I have earned? I cannot walk, can hardly move my arms, I cannot even wipe my behind! Look at my limbs and joints – arthritis has completely paralysed me. For all of my life I have lived according to the holy scriptures, which my mother and father read to me daily, even from when I was very young. No matter how much money, or how little, I have earned, I have never neglected to give more than a reasonable share to the temple. I have never eaten meat – never! Not even fish! I cannot name one person I have consciously injured or treated rudely.

Recently I sent for one of the most prominent monks from the Hase temple and asked him to investigate my previous incarnations to see if my fate might be the result of misdeeds in previous lives. He could find nothing that might affect my fate badly. In one life I was a monk, attached to the very same temple as he, in another I was a village doctor and continuously ignored my own welfare for the sake of the villagers and peasants. In a third life I lived as a hermit, ate only berries and other fruit and spent day and night meditating and reciting the holy scriptures. If such piety only brings me to this misery then I do not know what it is all worth. If I did not have my bonsai tree to look after, I would die; it is the only thing that makes my life worth living. See how beautifully it stands there in the sun with the branches reaching out to heaven as if in devout prayer. Every day for forty years I have looked after that tree, trained it, nipped its shoots and pruned its branches. That tree is my only happiness!

Those are exactly my thoughts! replies one of the others. For the past five years I have not been able to look after myself. My children are busy with their own lives and never visit me. After all I have done for them, they should take me home and look after me day and night. But they do nothing. I will also maintain that I have always sacrificed myself for other people and I have never received any thanks. As a youth I was attached to The Temple of the Great Buddha, lived like a monk and have denied in every way the desires of my flesh. During my month long ascetic practices I developed a clairvoyance which let me remember my earlier lives. Everything was clear to me, I could see how my happiness with temple life was only on account of the devout lives of numerous incarnations; in fact I have lived so purely that the merciful Kwannon himself appeared before me and instructed me in the ascetic practices and the correct procedure for temple rituals and finally told me that already after this life I now find myself in, I could be freed from the torments of further incarnations. However, that I should end my last life on earth as a cripple, I cannot find any explanation for.

In one life, many hundred years ago, I was a simple but honest tofu seller who, throughout his whole life, had passion only for minding that bonsai pine tree which stands over there by the cupboard and which fate, by its unique grace, has placed before me again in this life. I saw it at a temple market when I was quite young, only eighteen years, and I recognized it immediately from my previous life. And look how it stands there; it has lived for many hundreds of years and yet it measures no more than one foot from the roots to the crown. Far be it from me to boast of my own deeds, but if there is one thing I have succeeded in, it is that

I have looked after that bonsai and brought it to the condition it is in now.

The third man – the one with no legs – has sat completely hunched over during the others' conversation, as if asleep. Now he tries to sit up properly and joins the conversation with these words:

I fully understand what you are saying, my dear fellow sufferers. Like you I can claim, with an honest heart, that I have never harmed a cat or, for that matter, any other living creature. When I retired I gave away my whole fortune to the welfare of orphans and to the temples at the foot of Mount Fuji. And still I am sitting here and have lost both legs as a result of the most agonizing infection of the veins. Plus, one of my arms is paralysed. This life is meaningless. Good deeds are punished and pious living leads only to misery. Even the worst criminal in his prison cell has a better life than we. Look at the politicians who constantly bring people into new misfortunes and who deserve nothing but to be thrown into hell, and yet they live fine lives. What sense does it make?

After these words, he glanced lovingly at a little gingko tree which stood on a bamboo table beside him.

I received that tree from my father when I reached sixteen. My father received it from his father, who in turn had been given it by his father, who, it is said, received it from his father; the history of that tree goes back you that it stands exactly the same as when my father left it to me; not one branch has grown on it, not even a twig; I have pruned every shoot with exquisite craftsmanship as soon as I saw it stick its head out and when I die the tree will be passed on to my son so that he can look after it for the next forty years, and keep it in the same condition as it is now. How many families can boast of such a tree? Truly, I call that love for a living creature. If there were a Buddha would he not look after us with the same care and love as we look after our bonsai?

But today I have sent for Master Watanabe from the Zen temple in Kamakura. Many years ago, when I was still a young man, he explained to me some of the most complicated passages from the sutras; at that time he was already a mature man and today, as he approaches one hundred years, I declare that in the whole country there isn't a more clever and experienced man, when it comes to spiritual matters.

I wish to enquire of him about the deeper meaning behind the three of us sitting here bound and chained as we are, and if he cannot give a good explanation, which satisfies all of us, then I am prepared to drop all the holy teachings and, what is more, to recommend that everyone who can, live a life of lechery and sin!

The others laugh loudly and applaud his words.

Their laughter brings the staff in and warm sake is served to the three. A cheerful mood ensues and, with great expectations, they await the arrival of Watanabe-san.

After a while, the sliding door opens quietly, and Master Watanabe enters, bowing. He is much older than the three and very wrinkled; a small, sinewy man with a furrowed face, adorned with enormously bushy eyebrows which still have their youthful black color. He is dressed in a currycolored robe, his feet bare in his sandals. Prayer beads hang from his belt. With startling agility he moves through the room, bows before the three and sits in the lotus position.

Let me hear what your problem is, he says. I do not have much time so you must express yourself briefly. I have heard that you three devout and respectable old souls have begun to doubt even the Buddha's teachings. Tell me now, what has brought you to this?

The one without legs, who has successfully brought this matter up with the others, immediately elects himself as their spokesman before the Master.

Listen here, venerable Master, he begins. You can see for yourself the mess we have ended up in. We all maintain that we have lived sin-free, if not to say, praiseworthy lives, not just regarding our present lives but, so far as we can possibly investigate the matter, in numerous previous incarnations. Never have we strayed from the righteous path, in our faith or by our deeds. Now perhaps one should not boast about oneself but when we see how it is for others, who have lived in sin, eaten meat and have been drinking throughout their whole lives, then we ask ourselves is there any foundation at all in the teachings on karma!

Look at the humiliating existence we live here – no pleasure, no peace is granted us, we are tormented by pain both day and night! Our only happiness is to take care of our bonsai!

We have gone so far in our speculations on this that we are just about to drop the faith. Let us hear what you have to say!

During all of what was said the Master sat quietly before them and looked straight in front of himself with a faraway look, as though he wasn't actually listening at all. When the old man stops talking, the Master remains sitting like this for some time without giving any sign of replying. The three old men dare not disturb him.

But suddenly his face begins to change, the blood fills his cheeks, his eyes flash and he jumps up with the liveliness of a young man.

Is the answer to your question not standing there in front of your eyes perhaps? he shouts and points at the bonsai trees.

Life after life you have tormented the poor plants day in and day out, year after year, every single bud you have seen you have cut off! You have had nothing else to think of but to obstruct their growth! And now look at the cripples you have created! Do they not resemble yourselves? Are they not the most perfect reproductions of your self? And you doubt karma? You are the living proof of karma!

You wretched creatures, who think you have earned praise by your idiotic acts of devotion! You think you can obtain karma in the same way as you save money in the bank! You deserve to be reborn as rats not only twice or three times, but ten or fifteen times!

With these words he takes hold of a bamboo cane which is leaning against one of the wheelchairs and begins to beat the three of them ruthlessly and without restraint.

When the nursing staff come rushing in, the Zen Master has vanished through the sliding door and the three old men are all lying on the floor whimpering. They refuse to tell what has happened.

The next morning they ask the staff to plant the bonsai trees out in the park, and with plenty of manure.

Before the week has passed the three old men are dead. As no one comes to claim their ashes, the staff spreads them over the bonsai trees.

Well, that too is a form of manure! they say.

# RIMBAUD, THE HUMAN GOD

The wonder of Arthur Rimbaud!

No, not the youthful raver, but the man, he who went to Abyssinia to trade in guns and ivory, he who let himself dry out by the sun and let his skin burn black for simple gain, Rimbaud the avaricious, Rimbaud the slave-trader!

The Rimbaud I adore is the one who killed a worker by throwing a rock at him, the one who kept a black woman as a sex-slave in his backyard, the one who threw into the flames the work of another man's life: ten folios of meticulous anthropological records and maps, that's the man who receives my homage!

The Rimbaud who no longer lived on illusions and assertions, but actively fought under the banner of death and whose poems were no longer composed of words, but of bones and dry skin and desert sand. The Rimbaud whose feverish visions and unintelligible outpourings no longer came from absinthe and hashish but from gangrene and cancer.

Rimbaud, the man-god! Tell me the number of your slaves, let me stack your gold bars! Lend me your gun, let me kiss your burnt skin! Take me into the the desert, show me a baking sun that can burn all sentimentality and delusion in my life to ashes!

# A THIEF OF FATES

A man stole fates.

With a light pat on the shoulder, in broad daylight, he could remove a person's fate with no one noticing it. An apparently coincidental touch at the vegetable market, or in the cinema, and the person was fateless.

People didn't notice any change. Future regicides and pirate princesses were changed into tv-addicts and pub-crawlers, without knowing what had come over them.

Fate had intended for Ilselil Olsen a role as a revolutionary hero and the world's first female u-boat captain. Thanks to the intervention of the fate-thief, she lived an easy life as a cashier in a supermarket and a mother of two in a detached house in Brooklyn. The Democrats are my party! she often said and one day received a gold watch for twenty-five years loyal service.

Herbert Bastian Madsen had been earmarked by fate to be the archeologist who was to rediscover the vanished Indian civilisation, Cibola's Seven Cities. After being touched by the fate-thief he had to put up with a very down-to-earth existence as a caretaker in a high-rise in Baltimore. It was a thrill for him to fill out a lotto coupon and when things were really wild he took a trip to the local carnival where he showed what he could do in the shooting gallery.

The fate-thief developed a sixth sense for those people whose fates were worth stealing. On the street, at long distance, he could spot a person who had that steady and clear look which revealed him or her to be one of fate's chosen, and he could follow such persons for hours, yes, for days he could spy on them, until the chance to touch them on the shoulder presented itself.

When the fate-thief let his fingers slide over the fates he had stolen, he could visualize them. He saw fantastic dreams unfold and he realized that, with his thieving, he was changing the course of history.

The fate-thief saw that people were happier without a fate. He started to see his activities as a mission. He had to relieve people of the burden it is to have a fate.

The country changed as the peoples' fates grew fewer. More televisions were sold, more lotto was played: A flood of people went on beach holidays, even more bought garden grills and computer games.

The fate-thief started to sell his fates to TV.

Never before had such exciting films been produced. People sat glued to the television screen not knowing that it was their own stolen fates they were viewing.

The fate-thief became a wealthy man. He gained access to the finest circles; everywhere he went he saw his chance to touch politicians, princes, generals on the shoulder.

Looming wars were averted; the most frightening tyrants gave up their power and devoted their time to playing golf or dominoes.

After a few years of this, the fate-thief had created world peace without a single person knowing the true explanation. In the end there simply were no more dramatic fates left to steal.

The fate-thief was bored.

He turned to devoting his time to young, beautiful women. It became an obsession with him to steal their fates and thus deprive them of the love-life they were entitled to. Women as beautiful as Sophia Loren were married to road-sweepers as the fate-thief sat on his sofa at home, letting his fingers slide over their fates and enjoying the sex-episodes he had robbed from them.

In the end the fate-thief met his fate.

For many days he had tried unsuccessfully to sneak up on the grocer's doe-eyed daughter. It was as though she had smelled out his intentions; every time he entered the vegetable shop, she darted into the back of the shop. He followed her on to the bus; just when he was about to touch her shoulder she turned around facing him and gave him a subtle smile.

He must, he would, he had to have her fate.

One morning when he entered the vegetable shop there was no one there.

He walked about a bit and suddenly she was standing behind him. She put her hand on his shoulder and asked: Can I help you?

Did he notice a tiny pull on his shoulder? No, he noticed nothing. And when he left the shop loaded down with vegetables, he had forgotten why he had gone in there.

On the way home his attention was caught by the window of the kiosk. One magazine had a competition in which you could win a trip to the Caribbean.

He entered the kiosk and bought a couple of gossip magazines. He leafed through them excitedly as the shop-assistant rummaged for change. An actress had moved to Florida, a singer was being divorced. He must remember to buy these magazines every week.

Near his home he noticed a philately shop. How was it he had never noticed a philately shop so close to his house? He looked in the window. Perhaps one should start collecting first-day covers? Join the Perforation Collectors' Club, a sign said. He walked home with his head full of ideas.

At home he started tidying up. Sack after sack of fates were carried down to the rubbish container. What in the world was this trash he had been collecting in his tidy apartment? He had to make room for a shelf for stamp-albums and buy a new television with numerous channels. The gossip magazines showed all the programs.

The fate-thief had found a new life. Slowly, world history could start up again.

## IN THE IMPERIAL STABLES

In the imperial stables I was the litter on the floor. Who brought me in, in large and heavy carts, and who removed me, mixed with dung and drenched with piss?

The grooms brought me in and out. Singing, they spread me, and sighing from tiredness they scraped me up and carried me out. In return I offered them a bed after their labors.

Where did I come from, how long was my life? The field hands sowed me, the sun and the rain forced me to grow, until the day when the harvesters cut me down and stacked me. On creaking oxcarts I was carried to the stables where I was chopped up and brought in. Already the next morning my duty was over and I was carried out on the dunghill to lay fermenting for months until the oxcarts brought me back to the fields where I was spread. My life lasted a year, but it only took me one day to do my duty.

Who did I work for, who were my lords? The horses were my only masters. My place was under their hooves, and from there I saw them born, growing up, mating, fighting, aging, and dying.

I knew their names: Mother of the Winds, The Eight-legged, The Whirlwind, The Ghost of the Moon.

I suffered under the stallions' nervous stamping when they were lead to the waiting mares, and I heard the rude shouts of the stable hands mix with the roars from the excited animals as the covering took place.

I was the midwife who accepted the bloody foals and the slimy afterbirths, and I was like a child drinking the milk that dripped from the udders of those miserable mares who gave birth to stillborn or deformed foals.

I heard the shrill shrieks of the stallions when they were castrated, and I silently absorbed their shameful blood.

I saw the strongest stallions tear themselves loose and kick stable hands and riding masters to cripples, and I witnessed how they attacked each other with their knife-sharp hooves. I was their first victim, but in the end I drank their blood and sweat.

I saw the butcher lead weak and aging animals out, and secretly I longed for their blood.

Flies and beetles were among my friends; I listened to their humming and buzzing; they laid their eggs in me, and I hatched them in the dunghill.

And there were nights when in terror I witnessed vampire bats flutter around and select their victims and quietly and imperceptibly satiate their thirst with the blood of the proud animals. I was unable to relish the drops of blood that fell on me on such nights.

I was the only one to survive the fires; I nourished their raging fury and my lustful crackling mixed with the death calls of the horses. I was swept out as ash, mixed with charred bones and broken plaster. But when everything had been rebuilt and replastered, I was the first to be carried in. I lay between the newly washed walls and the odorous woodwork when the new horses were led into the newly built boxes, and I felt how they nervously trampled me down.

People forced me to witness everything from the crudest fucking to the most refined love-making; I was the bed for the stable hands' ass-fucking and for their forbidden love games with milkmaids and adventurous concubines. Even the Empress's slim back and pale behind have rested upon me, and I overheard her lusty sighs without telling anyone. My smell was that of horseshit, mixed with expensive perfume.

I came to know human justice. In silent protest I witnessed how thieves picked out and carried off the most exquisite animals, and the next day, on the dunghill, I had to suffer the mixing of myself with their crushed, criminal bones and their chopped-up flesh. The scaffolds and gallows were never far from the dunghills.

I heard the thunder of war drums, and I saw the stables being emptied of the strongest stallions. When the battles were over, I counted the few that returned. And I saw horses captured from the enemy led in and, seemingly without any loss of self-esteem, let themselves be stabled among the animals who had helped conquer them.

My greatest joy? The horses, the horses. Even though they trod me asunder and shat and pissed upon me, it was my great joy and pride to serve them, and I took pleasure in absorbing their juices. Never was I tired of my task.

My sorrow? That I never witnessed the tournaments, the parades and the battles. Never did I see man and horse become one. And never did I satiate my thirst for blood.

In the imperial stables I was the litter on the floor. My life stretched over a year, my duty was done in a day.

## PHOENIX

In a distant, magic garden, surrounded by a ten-foot clay wall, grows a grand apple tree which bears fruit all year around. The tree takes up more than a third of the garden. An old man lives in a mud-built hut, thatched with grey tiles, and guards the tree.

Well hidden in the foliage live three metal-green beetles, big as sparrows, who feed upon birds that land in the tree.

With strong pincers they cut their way into the birds' hearts and eat them. The rest of the bodies are dumped to the ground.

The cats take them.

The ground is covered with tens of thousands of colorful feathers. When the wind whirls them up, they look like fantastic, dancing birds.

One day a Phoenix bird lands in the tree to steal a fruit. It spots the beetles who are too afraid of the enormous bird to attack it, and it swallows them, one after the other.

From the inside of the bird's stomach, the beetles cut their way to its heart and eat it. The bird drops to the ground, stone-dead.

The old man, who lives in the house, walks out into the garden and finds the gigantic bird lying dead under the tree.

What a big and fine bird! he exclaims. I will carry it into the kitchen and cut it up and eat its heart!

But as he opens the bird to take the heart out and roast it, he finds only the three beetles. He carries the bird back into the garden. After a while, it ignites.

A yellow spurt of flame arises from its wound and sets both bird, tree and garden on fire.

Within moments everything is engulfed in flames. In an hour-long fire that can be seen from miles away, the garden is trampled down by a madly dancing firebird.

In the end, nothing is left but a thick layer of ashes. Then it starts to rain; big drops fall and change the ashes to an auburn porridge.

Buried in the mud lies an armful-sized, pale-yellow egg. In three times three thousand years it will hatch, and a new bird appear.

## IT SHINES FOR NOBODY

The moon is shining, yet it does not shine for you. The moon is not here for your sake. It is not here for the sake of anybody. It is dead. Still it affects you so deeply.

Likewise, the sun shines *upon* you, but you cannot claim that it shines *for* you. The sun is ready to burn you to death, kiss you with cancer, dry your skin and bleach your bones. You make no difference to the sun.

The Earth is there, spread flat under your feet, but you cannot claim it is there for your sake. You are not even a louse to the Earth. One day the Earth is going to drink you like a glass of milk.

You hear birds singing, but you know well that they don't sing for you. They sing for themselves and for each other. You don't even understand the stories they are telling, and yet you love their singing more than anything else. And had you not witnessed their flight, how would you ever be capable of dreaming of freedom? Yet the birds are ready to shit upon you.

As you see, you are surrounded by a team of dead players and ignorants. And how about your fellow humans? One day you are gone, and what will they do? Nothing. A few boo-hoo's, and you are forgotten.

Doesn't it make you wonder: What on Earth are we here for?

# NEMO ERAM. MARE OMEN

Nemo eram. Mare omen erat.

Mare omen *meum* erat; nationis mei impedentis praenuntians. Fluctus, spuma, lenis aestus; haec signa prima adventus mei erant.

Nox erat, æquori maris dormiebam, aciem effugiens, sine forma, sine gravitate. Ex nihilo ortus sum; unda subita gregem avium marinorum in caelum jecit; tum surrexi. Etiamnunc aciem effugiens, etiamnunc sine corpore autem *eram*.

Moliebar. Navis mare fluctuabam; nubes vela mea, ante me insolenter undas aspersi. Magnitudine et impetu auxi; cito vim meam omnino intellexi. Nullo resistante in plenam latitudinem maris me extendi. Patrem non habui, nec fratrem nec parem; nemo orbis terrarum imperium meum minari potuit. Adulter matris meae eram. Mare tremuit atque cessit; etiam luna et stellae me fugere videbantur.

Vastatio eram. Greges balænarum præ me agi, æsto maris naves contudi, et quum quiritatio remigiorum audivi, risi.

Ad oras perveni! Mugitus meus in montibus atque vallibus personuit, quum super terram volabam et terrorem omnino excitabam. Imbrem, grandinem, nivem, fulmen, tonitruum præmisi; eluviones me subsequebantur. Silvas mille annorum radicitus evelli, oppida devastabam, omnia quæ a homine creata sunt disjeci; montes tantum volutare, herba tantum evellere non potui.

Omnia exaggerabam. Solus orbis terrarum eram, ubique imagini vocis meae circumdatus; caelum corpus meum atque pulmo meus erat.

Plenus eram; furore ipsius defatigatus. In brevi tempore cecidi; mugitus meus in susurrum lenitem deminuebatur; postremum et ille mortuus est. Nil sine frigore immenso reliqui, et ubique vestigia vastationis meae videbantur.

Ita mortuus sum. Ut somnium etiamnunc summae maris

quiesco. Quamdiu mare in speculo caeli se contemplatur, imaginis meae gravidum atque renationem meam divinare paratum est.

Nemo sum. Mare omen meum est.

I was nobody. The sea was an omen.

The sea was my omen; an announcement of my coming alive. Ripples, foam, a quiet plashing; those were the first signs of my arrival.

I was asleep on the surface of the sea, invisible, formless and weightless. Out of nothing I appeared; a sudden splash of waves threw a flock of seabirds in the air, then I arose.

Slowly I started drifting like a ship; the clouds were my sails, and I plowed the waves like a proud bow. I grew in size and speed; soon nothing could stop me.

I was mighty. I stretched myself out in the ocean's full width, I had no father, no brother, and no peer. No one in the world could threaten my supremacy. I was my own mother's lover, even the ocean had to submit to my fury. At night I seemed to chase both the moon and the stars.

I was destruction. Herds of whales I whirled ashore, ships I crushed in the breakers, and great was my laughter when I heard the crewmen's desperate cries. My roar resounded in mountains and valleys when I whizzed over land and spread terror wherever I came. Rain, hailstorms, snow, thunder and lightning I sent before me; floods followed me. Thousand-year old forests I joyfully tore up by the roots, I devastated cities, everything that was created by man did I splinter; only the mountains were too strong for me to tumble, only the grass was too hard for me to tear up.

I was alone in the world. All I heard was my own echo, all I saw was the sea of air, my own body and lung.

Finally, I grew full and weary of my own rage. In seconds, I fell and my roar diminished into a slight whisper; finally, that too died.

Yes, I am dead. But still I hover like a dream over the surface of the sea. And as long as the sea mirrors the sky, it is still pregnant with my image, ready to predict my rebirth.

I am nobody. The sea is my omen.

**N E M O**
**E R A M**
**M A R E**
**O M E N**

# FIGHTING TOADS

I must tell you about fighting toads.

Fighting toads are ideal for small arenas. You can easily stage a match on your own breakfast table. You can start by inviting the closest neighbors, but the rumor that you are staging toad fights will soon spread and draw spectators from far and wide. The audience will watch spellbound as the two combatants sit still for a surprisingly long time, sometimes up to half an hour, staring intensely at each other, without moving, without blinking, until all of a sudden and without warning, they grab each other's torso like wrestlers and twist and twirl until one of them manages to topple the other and expose his soft belly skin. The winner will now use a small thumb of hardened skin or horn, as sharp as a nail, to cut the loser's stomach open, and his little arms and hands will work like cartwheels to tear the entrails out and throw them wildly around in the room, sometimes right in the faces of the nearest spectators. A terrible ending for such a small and seemingly peaceful creature.

As the audience wildly applauds the winner, and the owner of the unfortunate loser hastily carries the mutilated body of his beloved toad out, the champion sits pensively, seemingly unaffected, and licks his fingers clean of blood and the glassy, sticky remains of the loser's entrails. His reward will be a thimbleful of dried flies or moths.

Toad matches call for heavy betting. In those regions where toad fighting has become particularly popular, quite a few fanatics are known to have lost all their possessions, houses, farms, even their wives, when they lost self-control during an exciting match.

Let me tell you now about the most famous of all toad fights, the one between the two absolute champions, Dio and Diabolo. They were the two biggest toads ever to enter an arena and they both appeared out of nowhere at about the same time. They left behind them a bloody trail of savagely butchered opponents, and soon no one dared set his best toad up against either of them. To continue making money on the two beasts, the owners themselves were forced to bring toads in for the slaughter. Bets were out of the question no one would back the opponents so the owners made their profit from heavy entry charges. They carefully avoided that match beyond parallel which every fan of toad fighting dreamed of: the meeting of Dio and Diabolo.

In the end, however, there was no way around it. The demand was tremendous, and the amount of money that could be made on the betting enormous. Both owners would hate to lose their champ, but in the end they agreed to set the two monsters up against each other.

The big day came, the show was sold out at ticket prices previously unheard of, and the betting reached unknown heights. The pile of money got bigger and bigger, with everybody constantly raising his bet.

The two toads were placed in the arena, sprinkled with holy water for good luck, and lots of cheap incense was burned. The signal sounded that the match could begin. No one dared breathe. It was impossible to guess who would come out as the winner. The two giants were equally big and scary. They started staring at each other. They continued staring, without blinking, for hours. Neither of them showed any interest in starting the fight. They just kept staring viciously. Nobody left the building. No one wanted to miss the match, and no one wanted to miss his winnings. People were biting their lips in order not to fall asleep. They came to the point of starving, but still no one dared to walk out. They were all sure the fight would start the very moment they had left the room. They would wet themselves rather than dare go out to the toilet. The women came to pick their men up but were chased away.

Evening began to fall, lights were lit and the performance continued through the night. The next day came and went; nothing happened. People started fainting, and were allowed to lay there. No one touched them. Nobody would take his eyes off the toads. A week went by, then another.

People began to die. After a couple of weeks, there was not a living soul in the room, that is, except for Dio and Diabolo, who just kept staring at each other. The two toad owners were the last to die; they fell over on the floor next to the table where the bets were stacked. The tossing of firecrackers, which usually announced that a match had ended and a champion been found, was never heard.

This is where the story-tellers usually end their narration. No one knows what actually became of the toads. They just tell us that they survived everybody.

The exact circumstances are lost in the mist. Some say the match took place several hundred years back, others that it happened only a dozen years ago, or even less. Some place it in the murky suburbs of the capital, others in a remote mountain village, or in another country and other parts of the world.

There are even those who claim that the match between Dio and Diabolo never took place. That it is a myth, a symbolic tale about the never-ending conflict between good and evil.

I know better. Not only do I know that the story is true, I also know that the match is still going on. I happened to witness it, just a short while ago.

So let me tell you now about the day, a couple of weeks back, when I, during my perpetual ramblings, suddenly realized that I was very close to that mountain village near the border where some claimed the match had taken place. I decided to check it out for myself.

On my way up the mountain slope I came to a village which I soon discovered was occupied by mature women only. Not a man or child was seen. Strangers were obviously both a rare and unwelcome sight, and I was baffled by the women's reticence and complete lack of hospitality. When asked, they reluctantly revealed that they all came from the village where the menfolk once staged the famous toad fight. As the match dragged on, they had repeatedly tried to persuade the men to stop it, but they were just chased away, at first by coarse words, later by a hail of stones. Finally as they saw their husbands faint and pass away, they had given up and abandoned the village to move down to where I now found them. There was only one road running through their village and they explained that by following it I would come to their old home. They did, however, strongly discourage me from continuing.

You may go up, but you will never come back! they warned. No man who has followed the road up the mountain has ever returned!

With these warnings in my backpack, I began my ascent up the winding mountain path.

It took me two hours to reach the village. It was the last settlement before the border; only a narrow sheep trail was to be seen leading up to the crest. Already at a distance it was clear that the place was deserted. Not even a cat or a single chicken crossed my path as I drifted through the empty lanes. Barrows, tools and harnesses lay scattered where they had once been dropped, and when I looked into the empty houses, I saw a thick layer of dust over everything the women had left behind. I passed empty stables and pigsties still waiting for the animals who would never return.

Finally I discovered the house. A cardboard sign, bleached by the sun and rotted by the rain, was nailed to a tree and, between two naive drawings of a green and a red toad, one could still read the names, Dio and Diabolo. A number of old, rusty bicycles were leaning against the wall and two soggy boxes of firecrackers were placed next to the entrance door, which was still half open. I hesitated for a moment before I dared step inside.

It took a while before I got used to the dark. Then I began to distinguish the dozens of dark figures who were sitting on benches in the room. They were dead, just as the story told. Their clothes were mottled with mildew and a thick coating of spiderweb covered several of the bodies. Not a woman was seen among them, only men. I took a few steps to get a closer view, but I felt as though I were violating a shrine. I watched their haggard, dried-up faces. Here and there I dared wipe a veil of cobweb aside. They all had open eyes. Even in death they had kept staring with hypnotised attention. Now and then, when I was very close to the face of one of them, I smelt a vague stink of garlic mixed with the all-pervading stench of mould. It was as if they could come alive any moment, turn around and look at me with their bright eyes, open their cracked lips and say a few words, give me some advice as to the outcome of the match or invite me to place a bet. It suddenly seemed overwhelming. I stepped back in fear, but kept watching them. Some had had their hands and chins bitten by rats. Many were still grasping bills in their hands, as though, to their last moment, they had been thinking of raising their stakes.

On the floor lay two men who distinguished themselves by being well dressed. They wore thick gold rings on their fingers and in their ear lobes, and they had big gold chains around their necks. They were the owners of the toads.

On a small table I noticed a huge stack of bills, covered with dust. I could have taken the money and would have had no more financial worries for the remainder of my life, but I couldn't think of money right now. I had spotted the toads.

They were the biggest I had seen in my life. Enormous, like the dishes you serve tortillas on. They were placed on a round, green table in the middle of the room. I walked closer, not without a feeling of fear. My heart was beating, and I had trouble breathing.

From a distance they looked like glazed stoneware animals, but when I took a closer look, it was clear that they were still alive. Their warty skin was shining, as though they were covered with sweat. They had yellow eyes, and each was watching the other with the most hateful expression. I could see them breathe, but neither dared blink. It was impossible to decide which was Dio and which Diabolo. They were equally large and frightening. They could be siblings or clones of each other. I felt an almost irresistible urge to grab a chair and seat myself quite close to them and watch. The fight could start any moment, it might take less than a minute, and I wouldn't want to miss it. Then I remembered the women's warnings.

I took a few steps back. I thought of producing a sound, throwing a stick or a small stone into the arena, anything that might trigger the start of the match, but it was as though I was frozen. With great difficulty I managed to work myself back to the entrance and turn my eyes away.

Outside I was blinded by the daylight. I staggered through the empty streets and left the village behind me. The heat was overwhelming, and descending the mountain was almost as difficult as the ascent. It was late in the afternoon when I reached the women's village where I was met with disbelieving glances. Several women ran into their houses when they saw me. It was clear that they thought I was a ghost. They had seen me alive just a few hours ago, but in a place like this, time has lost much of its meaning.

It no longer exists.

# THE CITY OF THE FIRE ONOMATOPOETICIANS

The city of the fire onomatopoeticians was situated beside the sea but it's not known which sea. Not even which country the town is in is remembered and even the town's name has long been swallowed up in the mists of oblivion.

In fact I have a feeling that if I don't write down the story about this town, with its once so strangely gifted people and its dramatic downfall, everything will soon be forgotten forever.

The city of the fire onomatopoeticians was situated beside the sea; the houses were built of wood and tiles and in tight rows which meandered along the bay and up over through graceful hilly country. Nearly five thousand people had their life and business here.

Amongst the fire onomatopoeticians a particular skill had developed: to imitate the sound of fire. As in certain African countries, where every single child from birth is gifted with the ability to sing, dance and make music, so all the residents of this town had an inborn talent to speak like fire in at least one of its many sounds.

It is not known how this art started, but it is quite certain that it was passed on from generation to generation with great seriousness; some families specialized in prairie or wood fires, others understood the art of reproducing the rage of the flames as they devoured big buildings; some families bore names like 'The Campfire Family', 'The Burning Ship Family', and 'The Ten Thousand Sparks Family'.

Fire imitation pervaded the residents' daily life down to the smallest detail.

Instead of cradle songs the infants were lulled to sleep by the mothers' graceful renditions of the open fireside's cosy crackle.

A child was not baptized until the day it was able to imitate the sound of a tinder-box that ignites a pile of wood shavings.

Young men proposed to their beloved by imitating the sound of flames licking up along a stockade fence; the girls, on the other hand, could say yes by enthusiastically reproducing the fire's roar at the moment a building is swallowed up by the flames and transformed into a fiery ball, or say no by convincingly imitating the fire's hissing when sprayed over with water.

The monks in the town's monastery devoted themselves to year-long meditation practices where, in religious silence, they attempted to imitate the sound, inaudible to the normal ear, of a candle guttering out. Magicians secretly engaged in the forbidden art of lighting fires by chanting the sounds of flames in front of pieces of paper or wood-piles.

One of the fire onomatopoeticians' favorite stories was a description of the time the town's young people's choir was invited to the neighboring town to give a performance and, on that occasion, reproduced the sound of a bush-fire so convincingly that the fire-brigade, summoned by frightened citizens, poured water over the whole choir.

Another story which is often told was about a boy who developed a very special talent for imitating thunder-claps and lightning flashes and who built up a one-man show on the elements' rage which ended with the most convincing rendition of a lightning fire's destructive rampage. He interpreted this theme so dramatically that the uninitiated often ran out of his performances in order to take shelter, believing that a storm was just above their heads.

One day, during a particularly intense performance, the boy made so strong an impact, even on the forces of nature themselves, that a flash of lightning struck from a near cloudless sky and killed him.

A statue of this young hero adorned the town square.

Nobody ever sang. It wasn't because singing was forbidden; nor was it because singing as such was unknown, as the fire onomatopoeticians maintained normal relationships with the country's other inhabitants; it was just that the town's citizens were so taken up with crackling, roaring and crashing, that for them it was much more beautiful than singing.

Once a year the fire onomatopoeticians arranged a huge festival which attracted thousands of listeners from all over the country. Wonderful shows were presented, such as 'The Fire in the Library of Alexandria', and every year the festival ended with an imitation of fireworks so life-like that the audience imagined they saw whirling suns, fountains and cascades in the night sky.

The year the city of the fire onomatopoeticians went under, the biggest performance ever had been planned: 'The Burning of Rome'. Everyone in the town was to participate; the least talented were to reproduce the Roman populations' shrieks of terror and the roars of the wild animals in the arena.

The citizens studied their parts day and night. They got so involved with the performance that in the end they found themselves close to ecstasy. Then one night, only two days before the festival was to start, by a stroke of bad fate, fire broke out in the town.

That night the fire onomatopoeticians gave their final and most beautiful performance to a real fire accompaniment.

People woke from their sleep and heard the fire's roar outside their houses; they immediately thought that they were hearing the neighbors engaged in a full dress-rehearsal for the forthcoming festival and instantly started playing their own parts.

Wherever the flames directed a roaring and crashing attack on a building, they were met with a similar man-made sound from inside the house. If the fire had been able to comprehend it would have marveled at the sound of its own echo everywhere.

Never before had the fire onomatopoeticians performed so wildly and with such depth of feeling. If they saw a gleam of light outside the houses, or noticed the smoke pour in over them, they were sure that they were phenomena conjured up by the intensity of their own performance. Their joy knew no limits. When the horror of the situation finally dawned on them, it was too late.

Only a single citizen, a master fire onomatopoetician who had the distinguished role of presenting the fire's fury as it attacked the ancient buildings of Roma Quadrata, was in doubt.

Fire has never sounded like that, he thought as he listened to what he believed was the neighbors' rendition. They are practising the burning down of the House of Vesta, and I can hear their women busily attempting to repeat the Vestal virgins' screams of terror. But it doesn't ring true. Early tomorrow I must practise seriously with these people, he thought, and turned over on his other side and continued sleeping.

In this way the whole town was burned down.

By a twist of fate only one inhabitant survived, the only one who had absolutely no sense for fire imitation. It was the master fire onomatopoetician's son. At the age of seven he still wasn't baptized and was the family's great shame.

Only thanks to his lack of musicality, was he not gripped by that euphoria which overtook everyone else in the town and made them victims of the flames; thus, this one witness survived to tell the world how it happened that a whole town could be burned down without a single person attempting to put the flames out.

The art of fire onomatopoetics died out. None of its practitioners were still alive to teach the technique and, as the truth about the town's fate became known, royal bans were issued throughout the country against imitating the sound of fire. Soon the last people who had witnessed the fire onomatopoeticians' performances were dead.

Of course this was long before the times of tape-recorders and video-recorders. No record of this forgotten art has been kept. No one knows any longer how many hundreds of years ago it was that the fire onomatopoeticians' town burned down.

And I, who have traveled over most of the globe, maintain that today there is not a single person in the whole world who keeps alive that ancient art form once known as fire onomatopoetics.

# GHOST CHILDREN

A number of years ago it happened that nearly every evening, going on eleven o'clock, I heard terrible screams from children coming from an old, dilapidated villa at the end of the road. Some evenings it became too much so I went over and knocked on the door.

An old woman opened up. There are no children living here, she always replied to my worried enquiries.

And, as I never saw any children around the house, I had to believe her.

A time went by when the old woman was not seen.

So the door was broken open, in the belief that she was ill.

She was found dead sitting in a rocking chair. Opposite her, on a little wooden bench, sat two mummified bodies of children. Going by their clothing, and the condition of the bodies, they had been dead for over fifty years.

## THERE WERE COLORS

In the beginning everything was black and white. Cleanliness and simplicity ruled. All movement took place on one surface.

Surfaces slid across each other, into each other, felt and sensed each other, bowed each other's corners and edges, formed mysterious figures in silent and tender acts of love.

Writing existed. Everything was black and white; everything was still and silent.

The world was a sheet of paper. The calligraphists witness this state.

One day a raven flew up from the page and time and space were created.

Aeons went by. The raven was alone in the world. In order to provide offspring it pecked a hole in its breast and the color red was created.

Red was born of black. Rivers of blood filled the world. Hate and love were formed. Humans appeared.

The world was black, white and red. Malevich is a witness of this time, and Gerrit Rietveld.

The raven died. From its rotting corpse the color blue appeared.

The wind and the sea were formed. Longing appeared and clouds rushed across the sky.

Red and blue divided the world. Sky above, earth below. Fire here, water there. Albert Mertz saw this.

The raven's bones remained and formed the color yellow.

The sun was lit, song and music appeared and conversations could be held. Fish appeared and birds filled the air.

Everything was in clear color.

This condition lasted long enough for Mondrian to see it

and reproduce it

So began the colors' love-making, their pain and passion. Blue and yellow produced green, yellow and red orange, and red and blue lilac.

Green appeared and nearly filled the world; with it followed the earth's plants and woods – well, everyone knows what is green, but also the shadows and dreams, and with this color the birds gained utterance. Mammals appeared, and frogs and snakes. Whistler and Dewing are the only artists who fully understood this color, and Lorca, the poet, saw it, as did the absinthe drinkers.

Orange was born and brought with it laughter, lies and death.

With the color lilac, rain and melancholy came into the world; the silver sheen appeared and the moon was formed. The royal colors of purple and indigo arrived and the finest nuances began to appear: the color of peach flower, and the colors which appear on a corpse in the very first days of decomposition.

The creation was completed. The rainbow could be seen. The humans were in heaven. Loud was their singing, wild was their laughter.

People's happiness now calls the new colors forth. Their names are midalto, grist, serval, esket and bodal; only a short and vigorous blossoming awaits them.

With them it will be possible to see at night, people will be allowed to see themselves from both front and back; they will be able to see the consequences of everything, and with these colors all lies will be exposed.

Many things will change; children will be born before their parents, the barriers of time will be brought down so that man can travel in the past and in the future, the dead will rise from their graves and all prayers will be fulfilled.

Then fear and shame crop up; people are afraid to see themselves; they hide from each other and begin to want the lie back; in the end everyone goes around with their eyes shut.

The splendour of colors must yield to the dark. Colors which no one wishes to see are doomed to vanish.

And so the new colors fade, and are quickly forgotten; people once again dare to open their eyes; death and the lies return but now also the old colors fade away.

The rainbow goes out, the combined colors are separated, one by one the colors disappear.

Lilac vanishes, gone are melancholy and the night's silver twinkle. Orange is separated into red and yellow, thus all laughter ceases. Green is no more, the plants wither, the song of birds ceases, and dreaming is no longer possible. Yellow grows pale, music vanishes, conversations can no longer be conducted. Blue fades away, and red; sky and earth are no longer and the last human is gone.

The world raven reappears; no one knows for how long it flies about alone before it once again becomes one with the black and white.

Everything is gone.

Only the writing remains.

# THE LAW OF 97½ PERCENT

Now, I know that statistics are boring but I have an urgent desire to share my knowledge of the law of 97½ percent with you. I have the feeling I am the only person on earth who knows this law.

So what does it say, this law of 97½ percent?

The law of 97½ percent states that 97½ percent of all human communication is nonsense. Rubbish, babble, twaddle, drivel, blather, blah-blah, small-talk, call it whatever you want: it is nonsense and should be avoided.

The law applies to all forms of human communication. 97½ percent of all books are rubbish, 97½ percent of all radio is rubbish, 97½ percent of all television is rubbish, 97½ percent of all films are rubbish, 97½ percent of all newspaper articles, 97½ percent of all conversation, 97½ percent of all speeches, 97½ percent of all internet sites and chat rooms, 97½ percent of all songs, 97½ percent of everything that comes out of the human mind is rubbish.

Some say that pornography is bad, but no way am I gonna buy that. Pornography is not bad *per se,* but 97½ percent of all pornography is bad. Some say that pop music sucks, but, knowing the law of 97½ percent, I state that 97½ percent of all pop music sucks. Some claim that everything men say is stupid, but I say that 97½ percent of everything men say is stupid. And the same goes, dear feminists, for 97½ percent of whatever women say.

I might add that 97½ percent of all artwork is untalented, and that 97½ percent of all restaurants and cafés serve junk food. The law permeates all aspects of human life.

Do I sound pessimistic? Not at all. These are plain facts. It took me many years to find the exact figure. For quite some time I settled for 90 percent, but when the internet appeared, I started calculating again, more accurately, and I am now quite sure that

97½ is the exact percentage.

Do I hereby claim that 2½ percent of all human communication is intelligent?

Not at all. I allow that 2½ percent can be discussed.

Okay, I lied to you. I didn't really discover the law. There was one before me, another bookseller, who was the first to see it, but in the end he chose to forget it. Here's why:

Herbert Mayfield discovered the law of 97½ percent and opened a second-hand bookstore which he cleverly named *2½ Percent.* He wanted to deal with books that belonged only to the category of 2½ percent, and, do I need to tell you, Herbert was quite proud of the idea?

Herbert's store was right on the main street of a middle-size drive-through town that boasted a railway station and a Greyhound terminal; I won't reveal the name of the town, but I can tell you that if you have ever visited Merced, California, you have a fairly good idea of how it looked. Perhaps Herbert should have chosen a bigger city, with a larger intellectual community.

So, here now was a nice bookstore, on street level, with two windows, a door in the middle, and a hand-painted sign that read *The 2½ Percent Bookstore.*

It created a lot of misunderstandings, and Herbert found himself with a lot of angry customers. First of all, many came to him with the belief that everything in the store, including signed first editions and multi-volume series like Encyclopedia Britannica, cost 2½ cents.

I want this book for 2½ cents! a customer said.

Nonsense! The book costs a dollar, as is clearly stated on the endpaper!

Your store is called 2½ Cent. I expect to get this book for that price, or I won't hesitate to call you a liar!

The store is called 2½ Percent!

Well, in that case I want the book for 2½ percent of a dollar, which is still 2½ cents. You can keep the half cent!

The customer threw a dime on the counter.

Herbert had run out of arguments. He kicked the man out

of the store.

But that was not all. Whenever a customer came in and asked for a book which Herbert really didn't think belonged to the category of 2½ percent, he had to explain to the customer that the book he or she asked for didn't belong to the tiny percentage of books which, with some right, can be claimed to be intelligent. The customer was, in other words, asking for a book which, without discussion, could be discarded as rubbish. Herbert surely managed to piss a lot of customers off.

Herbert was called arrogant, a neurotic rat, an imposter, an ignorant—there was no end to the words and names the customers found to throw in his face.

What's wrong with Erica Jong? You're nothing but a fucking sexist! a woman shouted.

Herbert soon found himself with no customers at all. After a mere six months, he closed the store.

A couple of months later, Herbert opened another bookstore on the other side of the main street. He never had a decent book in the store. He could have called it The 97½ Percent Bookstore, but he found it wiser to forget about the law. Instead he called his new store Books Are Everything. Customers were lining up every day, and Herbert soon became a wealthy man.

A wonderful attempt to fight the 97½ percent of rubbish that fills this world had ended, and the law of 97½ percent was forgotten.

You and I know it, reader, and no one else does, but do we dare tell them about it?

## DEAN STREET

There is a lesbian brothel on Dean Street, where women meet women to satisfy their bodily lusts and seek similarly minded company. Seen from the outside, the house is just an ordinary brownstone. Nothing makes evident the kind of activities occuring behind the curtains. As far as I know, the place has no name. The doorbell signs are so old that they probably refer to previous residents; some of them can't even be read.

I have not been there, as I am a man, and men are not allowed in.

But I live in the loft next door, and daily I hear the sighing and sobbing, the crying and wailing of the women who are making it out with their paid partners.

I have heard what sounded like war cries and primal screams, and I have heard sounds I thought only men could produce. I have heard the whipping of naked flesh, and I have heard the singing of obscene songs and the shouting of rude phrases. And in the evening, when the street noise has died down and everything has become quiet, I have overheard low-voiced, intimate confessions, and the recital of sensual love poems.

And I have seen, from my window or doorstep, girls and women of all ages walk in, some as couples, for the house is also a love hotel where a pair of women can rent a room for a night, or just for an hour or two, but most of them alone; some looking like men, and dressed like men, others more than feminine in dress and appearance; some in their daily clothes, others dressed for fun; some looking deeply depressed as they approach the house, others excited and expectant. I've seen Gertrude Steins and Marilyn Monroes, I've seen Ingrid Bergmans and Farah Fawcetts, there is not a type of woman I haven't seen enter that Sapphic temple.

And I have seen them leave, sometimes relieved and

laughing, sometimes almost flying, very often blushing, and occasionally disappointed and in tears.

Many times I have smiled to myself at the sight of a girl walking out with her panties sticking out of her handbag, or openly carrying a whip, a badly hidden dildo, just loosely wrapped up in a towel, and whatever other pieces of equipment that may have brought her to this state of happy absent-mindedness.

And more than once I have seen an angry man try to enter the brothel to fetch his wife, sometimes being shown the door, sometimes succeeding in dragging the poor woman, crying and half-naked, with him.

And I have seen the women who work there walk in and out, white, black and Asian, some young and beautiful, others mature and motherly.

I know that any sound and healthy woman can work there for a single day or a week, or any period she may choose.

Some do it to get away from their man, some to get away from their woman, some to get away from their loneliness. Few, I think, for the money.

Would I like to be a fly on the wall? Perhaps, and perhaps not. I guess I am happy with what I see and hear from my hiding-place.

Every Saturday morning two of the women carry a bag of linen to the laundromat around the corner. I often follow them with my own bag of linen, just to inhale the smell of exotic perfumes which fills the laundromat when they unpack the covers and feed them to the washing machines.

Every day has its little drama. One Sunday morning (the brothel is open seven days a week), I noticed a discreet, handwritten sign in one of the windows which read: Closed today for a private event.

At eleven o'clock in the morning, almost precisely, a limousine with black windows appeared and parked in front of the brothel. That was the first and only time I saw one of those cars in our street. The driver, a uniformed man, helped an elderly lady out. She had the appearance of a European countess and, with her dark sunglasses, looked very much like Greta Garbo. I got the idea that this woman was here to celebrate what might very well have been her 80th birthday.

Throughout the day I heard her shout out commands. She was using a whip on the girls and, later, they were using it on her. Suddenly, sometime in the afternoon, it all became very quiet; then I heard a lot of upset voices. Hers was not among them. Half an hour later I saw her driver, assisted by two of the women from the brothel, carry a bundle out to the limo. Not for a second did I doubt that it was the countess, wrapped in covers, stone dead from a heart attack. Could she have asked for a better death?

Every day the next week I carefully checked the papers for obituaries of a rich, elderly lady, who had suddenly passed away under undisclosed circumstances, but I found nothing that could give me a clue to her identity. She remained a mystery.

One hot summer night, after having spent much of the day watching through the window the women sunbathing in the backyard, I lay on my bed, unable to sleep in the heat. A woman was singing *Pale Blue Eyes,* while strumming an acoustic guitar. I noticed how well this old Velvet Underground-tune functioned as a lesbian love song. Finally, well after midnight, I heard the door shut as the last patron went home. As quiet descended, I grew overwhelmed with loneliness. Like so many times before, I was left with the feeling I was the only man in the world, surrounded by women I would never be able to touch.

## THE CAPRICES OF THE MOON

The moon shamelessly mirrors herself in the gutter. “This is what I call beauty, boys!” she joyfully shouts to the passers-by. A cloud modestly covers the drunken harlot. “Another time I'll let you see her, but not this evening, not tonight!” The moon hastens on. As she tries to escape the dreary cloud she leaves the city behind and seeks the open land where she knows of dunghills with oily waters that are always willing to reflect her naked beauty and are happily unashamed of her drunkenness.

# THE LANGUAGE OF THE BIRDS

By mere accident, I came to understand the language of the birds. Half of it was scorn and half of it lament, what I had thought to be the sheerest beauty was nothing but hideousness, oh God, how had I misunderstood these sweet and lovely tongues! I walked away in despair but everywhere the birds followed me with their thousand year old grievances; a sparrow was once crucified, a shrike had had its wings torn off, a starling had once been held prisoner in a golden cage in a distant land, a flock of crows had been chased away from a cornfield by rattling scarecrows, dressed in black, and, as if these complaints from olden days were not enough, the birds went on with waves of insults and disdain; wildly chattering they confided to me that a storm bird had once been crushed against the surface of the sea, had it deserved anything else for its careless flight? And they laughed hilariously at a blackbird whose eggs had dropped out of its nest, that silly bird could surely thank its ugly voice for such bad fate, a pack of wild geese had been led into a deadly decoy by a lighthouse, why hadn't they just stayed at home instead of trying to cross the ocean, stupid birds indeed. I was next forced to hear about a crane which had flown into a high-voltage line, an ugly sight, I was told, but it wouldn't have happened if it hadn't been so desperate to sport its tasteless, red cap, there was no end to their scorn, one story was barely told before the next two or three started, there was not a thing they didn't want me to know and, before I knew it, my mouth and nose had disappeared and were replaced by a beak as hard as steel and black as ink, greyish feathers covered my skin, my eyes were blinking, and with a chattering voice I joined the noisy choir, for I too had stories to tell about scorn and disdain.

They gave me the name Semiramis, the one who is bred

by birds, and promise me, dear reader, if I peck on your window tonight, that you will chase me away and refuse to listen to my song.

# PEOPLE PASSING BY

If you look down any street of a certain size, filled with pedestrians, one or two of the passers-by can, statistically, be identified as dead people who are either in a state of ignorance of their situation or, in some pathetic attempt to deny it, still linger among the living, trying to resemble them as closely as possible.

It does not require occult insight to understand this; all you need is clear and unprejudiced powers of observation and, after a short period of practice, anybody can learn to distinguish a ghost from a living person. This was our philosophy, me and my wife, at least until the day I am now going to tell you about.

It was one of our quiet, favorite pastimes to sit on a bench or at a street café and watch the stream of people passing by, pointing out those who were dead. We would grab any opportunity to indulge ourselves in this mind game and, after several years of practice, we felt quite certain we were experts in the strange art of identifying these walking witnesses of life's shortness and vanity.

The dead are so clever at copying the looks and movements of the living that only small details reveal them. These sometimes show as an unexpected ecstatic behaviour of an otherwise pitiful existence or, at other times, as a dark and bitter aura which covers the person like a grey cloud, or simply as a way of walking and moving which just doesn't fit the kind of figure they have tried to create. In some way these persons simply look a bit detached from the whole they pretend to be part of, and that is how they reveal themselves to the skilled observer.

One day at the beginning of October, when gusts of wind announced the arrival of autumn and the coolness of the sun was appreciable, we were sitting outside an East Village café, enjoying a French onion soup and a glass of white wine and silently watching people pass by.

After having spent a good half hour in this deeply satisfying state of sheer melancholy, we noticed a tall, elderly gentleman with a grey moustache who seemed to have stepped right out of the middle of the last century. He looked unmistakenly like the Norwegian King Haakon the Seventh, but he could also have been the elderly Knut Hamsun. Swinging an obviously unnecessary walking stick, he walked at a brisk pace, just slightly unlikely for a man of his age.

Him! we both exclaimed, in low voices.

As if we had called him, he changed his direction and came walking directly toward us.

We had trouble breathing normally. If we were right in what we assumed that the man was dead (and we were, honestly speaking, not in doubt for a second) it would be the first time ever that a ghost approached us. It was an unexpected and indeed unwished for development of our hitherto fairly innocent pastime.

Excuse me! the man said, in an old-fashioned diction and with a slight, possibly Nordic, accent. Do you allow me to sit down?

It would have been impolite to refuse him, so we both nodded and signalled that he could use the empty chair at our small table. When he sat we got an odd feeling that the chair had been waiting for him from the moment we had arrived.

I notice that you take pleasure in watching the passers-by, he began the conversation. That has been my favourite pastime for donkey's years. Just watching human life pass by, humans you will never ever get in touch with. Who are these people, and what do they want? Never, ever will one learn. I have sometimes regarded this fact as a relief and, at other times, as a source of deep melancholy.

All wandering is pathetic, he continued. Did you know that the ancient Greek word for a wanderer is a peripatetic? Language sometimes contains the most remarkable wisdom!

More than two thousand years ago, the Eleatics, a bunch of hair-splitting, ancient Greek logicians, succeeded in proving that movement doesn't exist, yes, that it is quite impossible for it to exist. And without movement, no life, most people will agree.

Diogenes, the well-known Cynic, thought to deliver a striking piece of counter-evidence by simply starting to walk to and fro. Why, might one now ask, has this demonstrative evidence not gained the same kind of fame as Alexander's untying of the Gordian knot or Christopher Columbus' (or rather: Brunelleschi's) upright balancing of an egg? Because Diogenes' evidence simply isn't valid! One can easily get the impression that this endless stream of wanderers, who you take such pleasure in watching, have no other purpose to their lives and activities than to contradict the Eleatics as if the alarming statement of these ancient ones would prove right the very moment people stopped wandering but these people cannot contradict anything at all! I, who likewise take pleasure in a stroll, know that the Eleatics are right, and the sole purpose of my wandering is to prove their statement. Only the ignorant see movement as a manifestation of life. I can guarantee you that movement is stillness, made clear and visible. Life is death and that's it!

And as for logic, what can be more illogical than the fact that there are thousands of people, with whom you will never get in contact, and definitely never learn to know, who nevertheless allow themselves to walk by, in a never-ending stream, right in front of your nose! What is the idea? They are walking three steps from your very face and still your contact with them is virtually non-existent! In other words, they might as well be dead! And, trust me, in reality they are!

He pointed directly at my face with a long, bony finger and continued: And allow me now to claim that it has been your private little pastime to sit quietly, withdrawn from the swarm of people and proclaim some of these, your fellow beings, to be dead!

I moved a bit uncomfortably in my chair and cleared my throat.

Well, I must say you surprise me, and I wonder how you are able to know about this when you couldn't possibly have been listening to any of our conversations, but yes, I confess, you are perfectly right! But since you have taken upon yourself the liberty of contacting us and since you seem to know so much about us and about the dead I guess I can hardly offend you if I now claim that you yourself are one of those deceased who, for one reason or another, wish to maintain the illusion of belonging to the living!

Of course you are right! he exclaimed.

How long have you been dead, if I may ask?

A hundred years. Or forever. As you probably have understood by now, my experience tells me that life is but a shadow dance and death is nothing but its mirror image. Whether I claim to be a dead man who was once living, or whether I claim to be living and once dead, makes no real difference. So, you see, you are doing great injustice to both the living and the dead with this seemingly innocent little observation game of yours. It is not only those you take pleasure in pointing out as dead who are so, *it is everybody!* And mind you for this seems never to have struck you there are people present now who are actually watching *you* and making their judgments about you!

As he spoke these words he looked steadily at us, and both my wife and I jumped. Didn't the man just accuse us of being as dead as he, and as dead as all the passers-by we had pointed out as ghosts? And wasn't he saying that we, unknowingly and unwillingly, all the way through had been co-actors in if not to say *victims of* our little observation game.

Now I hope I haven't bothered you too much with my talking, our guest continued. Sooner or later, the pieces of the puzzle must fall into place. It happens to everybody, and why should *you* be spared?

With these words he stood up and left.

The waiter brought the check and I paid him. We glanced quickly at the passers-by. It was all too clear to both of us that we would never again be able to enjoy our once so pleasant and innocent pastime. We sat for a moment in despair before we left the table and walked off, hoping that no one noticed us.

## AN EEL MESSIAH

Anguilla woke from a strange dream. The sun had set, but the evening was still light and it made her feel uneasy. She hated the Nordic summer nights where the sunlight never really seemed to leave the air. It was now August, so the worst part of the season was over, but she still didn't feel comfortable with it.

At least the moon wasn't up. Anguilla, like all eels, loathed the moon. She had a built-in moon calendar which kept her informed about the phases of the moon and helped her avoid its eerie and ominous face. It was now the third quarter of the moon, and she had the whole night to search for food.

She couldn't think of food now, though. She had to try to remember her dream. Slowly, she began to recall it.

She was unbelievably small and floating in a warm stream of water along with thousands of other eels, equally small and leaf-shaped, and all sharing an immense feeling of bliss and balance, as if they were one living being. They felt neither hunger nor fear. The big white eel in the sky was leading them on their way, and they had no worries at all. Now, as she lay well hidden in the mud among the reeds in the small lake she could still feel some of the divine harmony, but it was fading and she feared it would soon be over.

A sense of melancholy and immense loneliness set in. Something beautiful had been lost, probably forever, and she didn't even know what it was. Her eyes were wet with tears. She was hungry but felt little lust for hunting.

She was a beautiful yellow eel, with small eyes and dozens of razor-sharp teeth. She was nearly five feet long, and weighed a full twelve pounds. European eels don't get much bigger than that and she had now reached the age where it was time for her to return to her birthplace in the Sargasso Sea. A journey that would mean the end of her life.

She slipped out of her burrow and started sliding through the grass. She could smell frogs and it didn't take long before she could hear them singing. A single one of them and she would need no more food this night.

She was a skilled hunter. Nearly ten years she had spent in the lakes and meadows of eastern Jutland, occasionally taking a stint up the rivers to the central hills and woodlands, but always returning to her own hunting grounds.

This evening nothing seemed to work for her. As she was sneaking up on the frogs she moved through some leaves and happened to make a noise, a most unusual blunder on her part, and the frogs immediately jumped back into the lake. She then decided to leave the lakeside and head for the meadows where she was sure to find an abundance of small lizards and snails, but tonight she stumbled over nothing but a couple of beetles feasting on a cow pat. It was after midnight before she finally was able to satisfy her hunger with the remnants of an old rat carcass.

She was lying still in the grass, digesting, when she smelled another eel approaching. Soon she recognized it as Sipho, a male of her own age whom she had known since they were both elvers.

Hello Anguilla, Sipho greeted her. Nice to sense your odor!

Good evening, Sipho, she replied. Good to smell you!

Nice, warm evening, huh? Sipho continued. A bit too light, perhaps, but still, we shouldn't complain. How have you been doing?

Not too well, I'm afraid. I've only had a couple of dung beetles and now this rat carcass. I'm not really myself tonight!

Well, you sure smell like yourself! Who should you be if not yourself?

I don't know. I had this strange dream, you know, where I was only a small larva. You may have been in it too, because there were thousands of us. I had such a wonderful feeling of harmony and beauty!

I guess you must have been dreaming of your childhood when you were carried from the Sargasso Sea by the Gulf Stream.

We eels have a good memory but it usually doesn't reach that far back.

Were we really so happy then? I wonder where that sensation of bliss came from. And I wish I could bring it back. I would give my whole spinal column just to experience it again.

Well, I must admit I can't remember a thing from those days. It's quite a number of years ago, isn't that true? By the way, you are so old now that you'll soon have to begin your journey back to the Sargasso.

I don't want to leave this place. This is my home, you know. I don't know why it is that eels suddenly want to migrate. Why can't we just stay here where there's plenty of food? They say we don't even eat when we migrate.

It's impossible to avoid. It's the law of life. You cannot fight against your own inner nature. The only eel that doesn't migrate is old Elonginus who is trapped in the well near the water mill. He can't get out so he is forced to stay. They say he is a hundred years old. By the way, he may be the one who can answer your questions about how the larvae feel. They say he knows everything.

I want to go and see him then. How do I get to the water mill?

It will take you two days and two nights. You have to go up river until you come to the bend with the lobster traps — see that you avoid the lobsters! that's where you go ashore and cross the meadows. Lots of snails there. Hide well in the daytime, because there will be human children playing. When you smell fresh water, you'll know you are near the small river with the water mill. Go upstream for most of the night until you hear the mill. Go ashore and you'll find the well near the edge of the oak forest. It smells of still water so you won't have trouble locating it. By the way, it is not in use so you don't have to fear humans.

Listen, I will start immediately! I can reach the lobster traps before dawn!

Yeah, but don't sleep in the water! The lobsters will take you. Go ashore and you will find a pond in the meadow where you can hide in the daytime. Still it is not the safest place on the planet, but if you really want to go you have to take the risk!

Thanks for your advice, Sipho! I'm on my way, but I'll be back. Smell you soon!

Smell you! And have a safe trip! Greetings to the old guy, he may remember me! I visited him when I first arrived here as an elver. I nearly fell into the well!

It didn't take long to find the river, and soon Anguilla was on a steady course upstream.

She followed Sipho's instructions and shortly before sunrise reached the lobster traps where she climbed a small dam and went ashore to hide in the pond in the meadow. The day seemed endless. She couldn't sleep and had trouble waiting until it got dark again. As soon as the sun was down and the grass was wet enough for her to slip through it, she continued her journey. She found the small river and hurried upstream. It was unknown territory, and she feared otters and beavers might attack her.

Finally, well after midnight, she heard and felt the splashing of the mill. Her heart was beating with excitement. She had arrived! She closed her gill slits and slipped ashore. The cool night air penetrated her skin as she began to slide through the grass towards the forest. Soon the smell of still water tickled her nostrils.

The well had not been in use for decades. It was overgrown with creepers which made it easy for her to climb to the top of the brick wall. She lay still for a moment and smelled the water. The thought of slipping into the well and never being able to escape, frightened her. Then she heard a call from down below:

Anyone there? I think I smell an eel!

It was Elonginus. His voice was deep and rough. She had never heard an eel with a voice like that.

She could see his head sticking up from the surface of the water some three feet below her. He was incredibly big for a male.

Elonginus! she shouted. I have come for advice! I am Anguilla, a yellow eel! Sipho sent me, who visited you as an elver some years back!

I remember Sipho! A bright boy! Hasn't he gone back to the

Sargasso yet?

No, Sipho is still here. He is my age and says it will soon be time for us both to go back. But I am not sure I want to. Elonginus, I have had this strange dream I want to tell you about. I was but a larva, floating along in a sea of bliss. There were other eels too, thousands! I want to return to that state, Elonginus. I don't want to go to the Sargasso!

It has to do with sex, said Elonginus. You have had the rare chance to remember a glimpse of your original state of perfect sexual balance. Few eels have ever had that experience, and it is quite dangerous because it easily leads to a state of melancholy and depression where you become more vulnerable to predators. It is necessary to forget your past or else the whole species will be in danger! You are a rare exception, Anguilla! I too, in my loneliness, have had that experience, in fact several times, but few else have. It is no threat to me, since I am stuck here and have no enemies.

What is sex, Elonginus? Anguilla asked. I am aware that I am female, but the only thing I know about the males is that they are half my size. You are the fattest and longest male I ever saw!

That comes with age, you see, and from the fact that here I don't have to share my food with anybody. Anguilla, you were once a hermaphrodite. An androgyne. Not a boy, not a girl. That is a state of perfect inner balance, and with it comes that universal joy you felt. All eels are born like that, but as the larvae transform into elvers, all eels must become either male or female, and the harmony is lost.

It is like losing half of your identity and it is, in a sense, a shame, but such is the law of nature. If we didn't turn into these half-beings that males and females are, we would never be able to breed and the whole species would die out. To live is to sacrifice, you see. First you sacrifice half of your sexuality and, along with that, your feeling of cosmic unity, and then, finally, you sacrifice your life. All for the sake of the species. There is a short happiness awaiting you which you can hardly dream of; it will be beautiful and in some way resemble the bliss of your dream, but it will lead directly to your death.

Death? That means I will not be here anymore?

Death. The end of everything. It comes to us all. Just like the frogs you eat.

So going to the Sargasso means death?

Definitely. No one ever returns.

I don't want to die! There must be a way to stop this! I want to go back to that state of happiness!

Forget your dream, Anguilla. It will do no good to long for something that has been lost. The processes of nature cannot be reversed!

How about you? They say you are a hundred years old, and you just told me you have shared that dream of mine many times!

It is different with me. I cannot escape. The big clock that rules the inner processes no longer ticks for me. You wouldn't want to live in a prison like this, would you? And I too will die one day. The only one who lives forever, and is both male and female, is the big white eel in the sky.

I want to tell all eels they must stay here and never return to the sea!

It is no use, Anguilla! As I said, there is an inner clock ticking. One day it will force you to go and that day will be coming soon, I can tell just from smelling you! There is no way around it. You must abide by the laws of nature! Tell other eels what you like, but they won't listen!

Anguilla said goodbye. She caught a frog in the grass which she dropped into the well as a gift to Elonginus, and then hurried off. All of a sudden it had become clear to her that she had a mission.

She swam directly home and didn't even bother to rest in the daytime. Going downstream was like flying, and the faster she went, the more excited she became. She wanted to save all eels from death. She wanted them to live forever, and she wanted to restore that androgynous harmony which she now knew was so closely connected with eternal bliss. A lot of ideas about how to reverse the biological clock went through her head. Praying, diet, physical exercise. She knew she would find out. But first of all: no more migration. Migration led to death. She sensed the presence of the big white eel in the sky, and she knew she had been carefully chosen for this mission.

Already the next evening she was back in her old habitat. She slipped ashore and her nose soon told her that the meadow was filled with eels. It was a perfect night to give a sermon.

She sought out a tuft in the middle of the field and nervously pressed herself down in the grass for a moment before she dared raise her head and began shouting at the top of her voice:

Come gather around me, all yellow eels and elvers in this field! Tonight is the night when the coming of a new world will be announced to you! A world without death, a world with nothing but happiness and joy! We eels are cosmic beings that from now on will live forever! I have found out the truth about life, about how we lost half of our identity and how we shall regain it! Male and female forms shall no longer be separated! The twain shall be one! That is how harmony is created! And with harmony comes eternal bliss! From now on there shall be no more fear and no more sorrow but one everlasting joy, and death shall have no dominion! Follow me, and I will free you from darkness! I will free you from unknowing! I will free you from the circle of life and death! Everybody who comes to me will have their primordial state of complete inner balance restored! Boys shall no longer be boys, girls shall no longer be girls, and no longer shall they mate! Because mating leads to death! Migration will stop and we will create an earthly paradise!

There is much more I have to tell you, but let this be all for tonight. I will deliver another sermon tomorrow night, so be sure to tell all eels you meet that they must come! This is the beginning of a new world for all eels!

There was silence for a moment. Then she heard a sharp voice call out:

Where in all the mud on the earth did you pick that crap up?

It is not crap! It is the truth! I had a visionary dream! It was explained to me by Elonginus, the old eel in the well! He is a hundred years old, only because he does not migrate!

Who wants to live in a well?

Believe me, death awaits you if you don't listen! Do you know what it means to die? Think it over! Die! Like worms and snails! Die! Like frogs and lizards! Who wants do die? Eels are not meant to die! Eels are meant to live forever! Once you spawn, you die! You know that this is true! You have all seen hundreds of eels disappear and never return! Only androgynes can live forever! Only androgynes can reach that blessed state of mind which I, Anguilla, have experienced! I am the chosen one! I have been sent by the great white eel as your savior!

What's the matter with you, Anguilla? Have you been staring at the moon?

I am not mad! The natural state of eels is androgynous! And to the androgynous state we will return if we refuse to migrate! We eels must join together and refuse to migrate!

When will the eels stop migrating? shouted one. When the Sargasso Sea dries up!

Everybody burst out in laughter.

Follow me upstream! Anguilla continued. There are dams behind which we can form a colony of non-migrating eels!

Do you really expect us eels to live like hermits? A large eel shouted. And you know very well that these dams are made by humans, our greatest enemies! They will trap us and kill us all! Tell us, whose side are you on, you sleazy snake?!

Anguilla was shocked and unable to speak. No one seemed to take her side. Even some elvers had shown up and began to scorn her.

Doesn't that girl stink! they shouted. She deserves nothing better than to be nailed to a fishing stake!

Yeah! Let the humans take care of her now that she seems to be so fond of them!

The eels drew closer and some of the biggest girls started snapping angrily. All of a sudden Apodia, a monstrous snake of a female eel, went right at her and bit off a good part of her dorsal fin. Anguilla screamed with fear and pain.

Yeah, bite her! Several eels shouted out in shrill voices. Kill her! She's a heathen! She might as well ask us to worship the moon!

She had to flee the scene. She careered down the turf and started whipping desperately through the grass, heading for the lake. A few of the other eels kept chasing her until they heard her splash into the water.

She dug herself deep into the muddy ground on the opposite side of the lake and stayed there for the next couple of nights while she recovered from the shock. She felt no urge to go out and eat, but an increasing feeling of restlessness made her feel almost desperately uncomfortable and one night this finally forced her to leave the burrow. Outside, no one took any notice of her, and the rough events of the other night seemed to be forgotten. She was meandering through the wet grass with no particular purpose on her mind, when she suddenly heard a call she had never heard before:

Hello, Bigeye!

It was one of the boys, Angustus. And it struck her how right he was. Her eyes had really begun to grow. She could see incredibly well. And more than that had changed. She hadn't felt hungry for a week. Her teeth were sore and inside her body there was a strange feeling, like a growing hunger for something other than food. She didn't know what it was but she was aware that this hunger was the reason for her restlessness. She was, in brief, getting sexy. More males approached her, in a way that was completely new to her. She was flattered by their naughty remarks and, to her own surprise, had a fresh, streetwise reply to each of their calls. It was not only her body, but her personality that was changing.

Life was becoming fun. It struck her that her whole life had been about nothing but scavenging. That part, at least, was over. She had stopped eating completely and was never to feel hungry again in her life. A couple of nights later, her teeth simply fell out.

Anguilla didn't know it, but she had turned into a silver eel. Had she been able to look inside herself, she would see that her intestines were deteriorating and her ovaries were taking over all the empty space. They were rapidly being filled with eggs, in the end totalling a million, ready to be fertilized.

It dawned on her that old Elonginus was nothing but a stinking liar. What he had been telling her about dying wasn't true. On the contrary, life had just begun! The old, deprived geezer was just jealous. That's what comes from living in still water! What does a prisoner know about life? Soon she had forgotten all about her dream.

For the next many nights the eels lived a carefree and jolly life in the meadows. They were getting ready to break up, and they were constantly joking about some, not too clearly defined ecstasy they expected the migration to bring them. And one night, as Anguilla and some other girls were fooling around in the wet grass with the boys, one of them suddenly shouted out: Hey! Why don't we start out tonight? The moon is down!

Another one immediately replied: Me for the waters! and off they all went. Hundreds and hundreds of eels of both sexes flocked to get into the streams that led to the ocean.

Led by magnetic currents, and by their newly gained eyesight, they navigated with great confidence through the Danish straits and sounds, heading north around the peninsula of Jutland which lay as a great barrier across their route, and, without losing their sense of direction, they poured into the North Sea. They passed the white cliffs of Dover and entered the Channel. The voyage would last four months and take them nearly 4,000 miles across the Atlantic Ocean. They were on their way to the Sargasso Sea.

They spent the whole winter traveling, only disrupted by the regular appearances of the full moon which forced them to seek shelter at the bottom of the ocean. Finally, in June, their journey came to an end. One early evening, Anguilla suddenly noticed an unusual smell. It only took her seconds to recognize it, even though it was 10 years since she last had sensed it. It was the smell of Sargasso Weed.

I have come home! she cried.

Other eels had already arrived, and the water was soon thick with their eggs and sperm. It was a giant new-moon spawning party, and Anguilla was just about to take part in it.

The smell of the ejaculations excited her so much that she lost all self-control. Her heart was beating fiercely and her whole body felt like fire. She was ready to burst, and so she did. She threw herself senselessly around, bathing in sperm, as she literally exploded and hundreds of thousands of eggs poured out of her. It was an orgasm. It was the most beautiful moment of her life.

It is fulfilled! she cried in excitement. She no longer recognized anything around her. Her brain had stopped functioning.

It was a question of less than ten minutes before she lost consciousness completely and her empty, hollowed body started drifting randomly around amongst hundreds of all kinds of fish that were flashing through the water, feasting on the nourishing soup of gametes. That night, less than two hours after the happiest moment of her life, Anguilla the eel died.

The next morning her body was found floating among the brown Sargasso weed by a couple of sea otters who immediately began to rip her apart and eat her like a sausage. It was the meat of a failed Messiah they were devouring, but little did they know and little did they care. The sea had seen it all happen before, millions of times, so it didn't care either. And the big white eel in the sky was not present to witness the scene, since it was daytime. And even if he/she had been there to watch, the sight would have made no impression on him/her. He/she would soon be busy guiding thousands of newborn eels to the distant shores of Europe and America. They would be androgynes, but only for a while, before their own hormones would castrate them into single-sex beings.

And, as regards Messiahs, life runs in circles and nature doesn't care at all for individuals who suddenly get the idea that they want to break these eternal cycles.

It is perfectly happy to see them die.

# OLD MAN

His name was on the door. Just the surname, no initials. I don't know why it surprised me so much that it nearly scared me off.

I paused for a moment before turning the doorknob. The door was unlocked, and I walked in.

I found myself in a living room with an open fireplace to the right and a wall of shelves to the rear, completely filled with folders. This room obviously served also as his archive.

And there he was himself, sitting, hunched over at a table, with his back to me. A walking stick was leaning against the table. He was reading a recent issue of *The New Yorker.* He turned around and looked at me. I recognized his long, horse-like face, with the broken nose, and the thick lower lip which revealed his Jewish blood. He was old now, but still looked impressive. His hair and eyebrows had turned white but his black aura hadn't left him. He looked at me, without saying a word. He could have chased me off, but he didn't even ask who I was. Was he senile? Unable to talk?

No, it didn't seem that anything was wrong with him. I had the feeling that he had actually been expecting me and knew what I was about to do and that he had no objections.

I started walking towards the shelves. My feet felt heavy as lead, and I could hardly breathe. It seemed an hour's walk just to reach the rear wall where the folders stood meticulously arranged on the shelves. Each folder had a title written, in a firm hand, on the spine. Some seemed to contain diaries, others held comments on different authors' works and even on a variety of everyday subjects. There were commentaries on the Vedanta and on Buddhistic moralistic ideas, but most of the folders contained short stories. Dozens and dozens of them. Some titles suggested he had been writing crime fiction, and there were more Seymour stories, and even another Caulfield novel.

I picked out a particularly thick folder and threw it into the fireplace. It nearly put out the fire, and I realized that I had to open the folders and spread the pages in order to make them burn.

He made no attempt to stop me. He just sat and looked at me. Not a single emotion stirred his face. Perhaps his eyes turned a bit more sullen.

It took me more than half an hour to empty the shelves. The room became incredibly hot. The flames lit it up and threw dark shadows over his furrowed face, making him look even more haggard. I walked into the other rooms to see if more manuscripts were stored there, but found only shelves with hundreds of books and an odd-looking cabinet which I guessed was an orgone box.

I returned to the living room and gave him a final glance. I had been very afraid of him, and I still was, even now when my mission had been accomplished.

Then, finally, he spoke.

Do you feel better now? he asked.

Yes. I think I feel better.

You might at least tell me your name.

You can call me Holden, I replied.

Okay. He nodded.

Are you going to write again?

No. It's over now.

I didn't say goodbye. I just walked out the door and closed it behind me. For a moment I thought of stealing the door sign. Then I turned around to head off. It was getting dark and it had started to snow. I walked to the edge of the forest where I stopped to look back. The living room was still illuminated from the raging blaze in the fireplace. I watched the snow slowly fill my footprints, and then finally walked away.

# THE KEY

So, dear reader, you now hold the key to my cell.

Do me a favor: throw it away. Forget you ever kept it. Throw it into a volcano, or throw it into the sea. Or just drop it in the nearest sewer.

You will never find another door where it fits, and I don't want my door opened again.

www.ingramcontent.com/pod-product-compliance
Lightning Source LLC
LaVergne TN
LVHW050943080826
845145LV00004B/1383

* 9 7 8 0 9 8 2 5 4 6 2 2 2 *